Just A Little Terrible

Vincent V. Cava

Edited by

Defne Güçer

vincentvenacava@gmail.com

Defne

I couldn't have done this one without you.

THE AUTHOR

Vincent V. Cava

His tales have been known to induce seizures in small children. Merely skimming through one of his stories can lead to anxiety, nausea, and internal bleeding. You should not read anything written by him if you are currently pregnant or nursing (including this author's bio...although it's probably too late by now). He's a man whose mind is so dark, not even the World-Wide-Web could contain his horrific imagination.

He is Vincent V. Cava!

The son of NASA researchers, Vincent V. Cava's writing has quickly amassed a following over the Internet. His stories have been translated into dozens of different languages and have been used to promote major studio films. You can find out more about Vincent by following him on Facebook, Instagram, or Twitter. You may also follow him on his mailing list for FREE exclusive stories and promos.

Table of Contents

FOREWORD

When you're learning to swim, the last thing you want to do is dive headfirst into the deep end of the pool. You need to wade into the shallow end before you get into the fancy stuff. That's why I began writing flash fiction before I started working on short stories, novellas, full-length novels, and screenplays. However, as my writing continued to improve, I never stopped enjoying the short stuff. There's something extremely satisfying about a good piece of flash fiction. It's like treating yourself to a scrumptious pastry halfway between breakfast and lunch.

I looked at this little project as an experiment. Can I scare you, blow your mind, or at the very least entertain you in a thousand words or less. It's quite the challenge. Writing in this format gives you little room to set the mood or introduce characters. In a way, it forces the reader to dive into the story headfirst. There's no time to wade in.

I'm proud of these tiny tales of terror and I'm happy to share them with you. From a creative standpoint, some of them took just as much planning and focus as many of my longer stories. I hope you enjoy reading this book as much as I enjoyed writing it.

SCHIZO

Donny Polk sat upright in his bed, back against the headboard as terrible memories of his childhood began flooding back to him.

Memories about the Bird Woman – the creature his diseased mind had conjured up during his youth. The thirty-nine-year-old family man was no stranger to schizophrenia, though he hadn't felt its symptoms since he was a boy – before his doctors had put him on a plethora of anti-psychotic medication.

He remembered the way The Bird Woman would wake him in the dead of the night, her slippery, forked tongue sliding into his ear, wriggling and writhing like some sort of alien parasite attempting to invade his brain. He could still vividly recall the way her breath always smelled of rotten meat, how its stench would rape his mouth, leaving its rancid flavor in the back of his throat every time she leaned her face into his and whispered her awful secrets. Secrets that appalled him as a young boy, that terrified him even more than her hideous, warped face.

He glanced over to his wife, Gina, who was sound asleep next to him in bed. Donny hoped a familiar sight would somehow snap him back to reality. She looked so peaceful as she dozed; her tranquil slumber uninterrupted by the panic attack her husband was currently experiencing. He felt as though he was losing his grip on reality. Gina was real. That much he was sure. What he wasn't sure about was whether or not The Bird Woman hovering at the foot of his bed was real too.

It was the first time he had seen her in three decades, but she was just how he remembered her – pale white skin, stringy black hair, and a pair of mustard yellow eyes that's perverse stare made Donny feel both terrified and unclean at the same time. His old nightmare had finally found a key to the vault in his mind and now she was free – unleashed for the first time in years and back for vengeance.

The Bird Woman lifted her leg and placed a deformed foot on top of his bed. Her black, crust-covered toenails left grime and dirt on his Egyptian cotton white sheets. Donny's heart skipped a beat as he watched the creature slide a second filthy, grotesque appendage on top of his mattress. She was coming for him – just like when he was a child. He considered waking Gina, who was still snoozing next to him. His wife knew about his history with hallucinations, but had never seen him have an actual breakdown. Donny wasn't sure how she'd react. The Bird Woman crouched on top of his legs like a wild predator stalking a wounded animal. Horrible whispers had begun to trickle out of her disfigured mouth.

His meds!

How could he have forgotten about them?

Donny remembered that he always kept a bottle of Clozapine in his nightstand just in case his hallucinations ever returned while he was in bed. He opened the drawer and rummaged through the darkness, frantically searching for the anti-psychotics while the Bird Woman started to slink up the bed. The smell of rotten meat began to force its way up his nostrils. Donny held his breath in an effort to prevent the repugnant stench from entering his lungs.

The Bird Woman was half way up his torso now. Her grubby claws nipped playfully at his crotch as Donny hunted for the drugs. The whispers had gotten louder even though the awful creature's lips weren't even moving. Donny tried to calm down by reminding himself that the monstrosity was just a product of his mental illness, but she seemed so real. The desperate man's fingers grazed up against a plastic cylinder inside the drawer. He had found what he was looking for!

Donny yanked the pill-bottle from the nightstand and unscrewed the cap. The creature's chin was resting on his chest. Her forked tongue hung from her mouth, snaking back and forth across the base of his neck as if it had a mind of its own. He poured a handful of pills, not bothering to worry about the recommended dosage as Bird Woman's slimy tongue slithered its way up the side of his face. The smell of her putrid breath had become overpowering.

With one eye trained on the monstrous sight, Donny raised the fistful of pills to his mouth, but felt a tug on his arm, giving him pause before he had a chance to pop the drugs. He turned his head to see his wife, Gina, eyes wide and full of panic, looking back at him. She swatted at her husband's hand, causing the pills to scatter across the bedroom floor.

The Bird Woman's gaze stayed fixated on Donny as she lapped at his cheek like a child with a melting Popsicle. Gina opened her mouth to speak, voice quivering between her lips. Her words would send a new wave of horror through her husband's body, the likes of which Donny Polk had never felt before.

"Donny," Gina whispered. "I see her too."

FATE

At that moment Jessica seemed so sweet and innocent. Her blond hair glistened like gold as the little bit of sunlight that had seeped in through the boarded up windows caught her curls. Her rosy red cheeks, so flush and full of life, radiated a warm glow in the dimly lit room as enchanting and captivating as any of Mother Nature's most awe inspiring phenomena. *Truly*, Michael thought to himself, *she was the most beautiful little girl in the world.*

He admired his daughter one last time as he raised the gun to her head. The shot roared through the house like a thunderstorm. Skull and brain fragments flew through the air as his daughter's carcass slumped to the ground in a broken heap. Carefully, Michael dragged Jessica's dead body across the floor, and laid it next to her mother and brother's corpses. A tear escaped his eye, but before the grief managed to overwhelm him, he took a deep breath and said a prayer to compose himself. It would all be over soon.

Michael peered out the 2nd story bedroom window of his home. Hoards of the infected stretched as far as his eyes could see and he knew that it was only a matter of time before they would blow through his home like a plague of locusts. Many of them had already made it inside and his bedroom door was beginning to buckle as the banging on the other side of it grew louder. It would not be long before the monsters broke through. He looked into the chamber of his revolver. Jessica had received his last bullet. The final gift a father could give his daughter. And as horrible as it was, at least his family had escaped his fate – the fate that would be crashing through his door at any second.

IMMORTAL

"What you seek is just beyond this door, young man."

Young man.

No one had called David young in a decade. Those were words that harkened back to a simpler time for him – before his obsession with immortality began to consume his life. Before he had wasted his physical prime locked away in his den, poring through archaic texts and studying ancient hymns. Before he devoted his life to investigating the validity of age-old legends from bygone cultures around the world.

From the Philosopher's Stone to the Fountain of Youth, David had researched tales of eternal life stemming out of every corner of the globe. He had even focused his efforts on more obscure, lesser-known lore, like the Owanu Frog of Ghana's Sisaala tribe and the disturbing story out of Slunj, Croatia that had come to be known regionally as The Night of The Star Child.

It wasn't until he reached his mid-forties that he was able to piece together a trail of evidence that gave his quest direction. He had begun to recognize patterns throughout his studies of history – tiny consistencies buried in long-forgotten writings, reoccurring symbols carved into timeworn relics, peculiar regularities that had no right turning up in the places and times that they did. And after more than two decades, all of his findings had led him to one place – a lone monastery sitting atop an icy mountain in Eastern Tibet.

David had braved the conditions in order to speak to the wise holy men he believed held the secret he had spent most of his adult life searching for, but when he arrived he found the temple mostly empty, save for one old monk with tired eyes. Pangs of disappointment surged inside the gut of the frustrated traveler when he first laid eyes on the elderly hermit. After all, he had come so far and been so sure that the monastery housed the key to his deepest desire, but the deep age-lines in the old monk's face told him a different story. It told the story of muscle atrophy, the story of cognizance withering away, of bones becoming brittle. The old monk's face told the story of aging – the story of impending, unstoppable death.

With a pair of wrinkled, weathered hands, the hermit seized David by the arm, and led him inside, away from of the cold. The entrance hall of the temple was barren. A row of torches lined the interiors' gray, stone walls providing only just enough light to illuminate the path ahead of them. The old monk, still clutching tight to his new guest's arm, began to hobble down the dim, corridor. Together, the two navigated through the darkness in silence, until they reached a winding staircase plunging downward into the monastery's shadowy depths. With his free hand, the elderly man removed the last torch off the wall and gestured towards the stairway.

"What exactly is this place?" David had asked the holy man as they began their descent.

But the old monk said nothing. Instead he directed his gaze ahead, his tired eyes focusing on nothing but the twisting steps in front of him. David felt alone as they snaked their way into the abyss – like a tiny rock floating by itself in the vacuum of empty space, millions of miles removed from the closest celestial body. The pangs of disappointment he had been feeling just minutes earlier had begun to mutate into something else entirely. Paranoia, angst, and dread were now running rampant inside of his head, weaving themselves into an indescribable terror.

Just when he thought the black void he had found himself in would drive him mad, a golden radiance caught David's eye. As the two proceeded closer to it, the source of the glow became clear and David realized that his research had not been in vain. The base of the stairs came into sight. They appeared to open up into a small chamber with nothing but a large red door built into the wall. Beautiful ornate symbols were inscribed into the face of it. Egyptian hieroglyphics, Sumerian designs, and a variety of other ancient multicultural characters lined the perimeter of the impressive structure. By the time they reached the bottom step, the old monk's torch was no longer necessary. A brilliant light was seeping out of every crack in the door, flooding the chamber in a golden hue.

The old monk released David's arm and raised a wrinkled weathered hand towards the shining spectacle before them. It was here that he uttered those words – those words that had harkened back to a simpler time for the explorer.

"What you seek is just beyond this door, *young man*".

"Just beyond this door," David repeated.

A rush of excitement swelled through him. He had found it. He had succeeded where Ponce de Leon and thousands of others like him had failed. He had located the secret to immortality.

David reached for the handle of the door, and with a quick tug, jerked it open. A blinding light burst forth, enveloping the room, swallowing David and the elderly holy man. He fell to the floor clutching at his chest. As the light intensified so too did the searing pain he could feel in his heart. It was as though the entire core of his body had caught fire. The pain was unbearable – the most excruciating thing he had ever experienced in his life.

Questions started whirling through his head. *What is going on? How could it feel so horrible?* He had never once read, in all of his studies, that the youth rejuvenation process would be a painful one. Something had to be wrong.

Summoning every last ounce of strength, David crawled along the ground until he reached the door. He propped his shoulder up against it and drove his feet as hard as he could into the ground, in an attempt to force it shut.

With a *THUD,* the door snapped closed causing the blinding light to disappear behind it, and leaving only a golden glow to wash over the room again. Down on the floor again, David rubbed his eyes while he waited for the pain in his chest to subside. When his vision had regained focus, he looked up to scan his surroundings. What he saw ignited an inferno of terror that burned mercilessly inside of his body, spreading like wildfire.

Looking down on him was a familiar face – one he had watched age in the mirror every single day of his life. *His face* – and it was sporting a satisfied smirk. He was somehow staring up at himself as if another person was wearing his skin like a costume. Shock and confusion overran his mind. No longer able to gaze upon the imposter he attempted to bury his face in his palms, but when he peered down, the sight sent pulse after pulse of panic through his very essence. His hands were no longer his, but he knew he recognized them. They were wrinkled and weathered. Hands he had seen before – hands that once belonged to an old monk with tired eyes.

GRAVE DIGGER

Digging a grave is hard work – mentally and physically exhausting. Oh, you thought it was just mindless labor performed by simpletons? Well, think again. You have to have balls of steel out here in the graveyard! Not everybody is capable of spending hours digging plots in the dead of night.

Why, don't be surprised if on a moonless evening with nothing but a rusty old lantern to illuminate this necropolis, you start hearing voices whispering from the shadows. What will you do then? Run away crying with your tail tucked between your legs?! Not me! Not when there's work to be done!

It's particularly difficult to bury a loved one. Many members of my family have made *this* the place of their eternal slumber. And who do you think is shoveling the dirt, eh? I'll give you a hint. It's not the Dalai Lama!

That's what I'm doing here tonight. Putting another loved one to rest – my mother to be precise. I told myself I wouldn't cry when I began digging this stinking thing, but I just can't help it! It's so hard knowing that after I pour this last shovel full of soil atop her plot that she'll be gone forever. Life's too cruel! I'll probably just wait around for a while after I'm done and reminisce about good times, you know? At least until she runs out of oxygen...

THE OLD HOUSE

As a child, I always heard whispers about the old, run-down house in the woods outside of town. Rumors of ghosts, ritual murders, cults and mass suicides floated between the mouths of chatty locals for as long as I can remember. Many believed the place to be abandoned, but there were those who told tales of strange shadows that sometimes danced in the windows. Others swore they heard voices echoing out from behind the walls of the dilapidated structure when they passed by. The story I'm going to tell you is about my experience with that place. I never saw specters frolicking in the darkness or heard the ghastly wail of some menacing phantom, but the events that unfolded that sunny afternoon still scare me just the same.

It was warm that day. The sun broke through treetops above our heads, scattering down to the forest floor, glimmering like golden confetti. I was twelve at the time. Peter was only nine, but even at that age my little brother seemed to be on a constant mission to prove his bravery to me – as if he felt it was the only way to validate himself in my eyes. We trudged through the last of the brush until we made our way into a clearing where the old house stood. We had both heard stories about the place before, but this was the first time either of us had ever actually visited it.

The derelict old building was an intimidating sight. Moldy rotten wood covered the face of the home like the diseased skin of a leper. Some of the windows had been smashed out while others were covered in a thick brown coat of dust. The house's entire frame crooked off to the left at an angle so sharp it seemed as if it was going to collapse at any moment.

"There it is," I told him. We stood at the edge of the clearing for what felt like an eternity, the two of us just staring at the time-damaged relic. "You don't have to go in there, Peter."

My younger brother sent a frustrated scowl in my direction.

"I'm not afraid."

"I didn't say you were."

"I'm going in there – all the way in the basement," Peter said matter-of-factly. "And when I do, you're gonna tell all the kids at school tomorrow how brave I am."

He puffed out his chest and marched up the steps to the front door. I'll never forget the look on Peter's face when he turned back around and waved to me just before disappearing through the slanted doorway. He was so proud. I took a seat on the grass and leaned my back against a tree to wait for him. An hour passed and still there was no sight of him. By the time the sun had started to set and Peter still hadn't returned, I could feel anxiety beginning to build inside of me.

What if the rumors were right?

What if a family of cannibals lived inside of that place and they were already preparing my brother for dinner? What if a monster was hiding in the basement, waiting to tear Peter to shreds as soon as he set foot inside? I wanted to check on him, but I was far too afraid to go into the old house myself. So I waited.

My brother finally emerged from the broken-down building just before the sun had set for the evening. Needless to say, I was relieved. I couldn't help but notice the curious expression on his face when he approached me – almost as if he was sizing me up for the first time.

"What took so long, Peter?" I asked him. "I was worried you got hurt!"

"Sorry. I lost track of time." His voice was flat and expressionless. Its very tone made me scrunch my face in discomfort.

I brushed it off and grabbed him around the arm. "Come on. We need to be home before it gets dark or Mom will ground both of us."

My mother gave us a stern lecture about staying out after dusk when we got back. The night went normally enough, but Peter's demeanor remained cold and distant. I had been curious to ask him about the house, but I didn't want to do it in front of my mother and father. We shared a room so that evening when we were getting ready for bed I decided to prod him.

"So, Peter?" I said when I walked into the bedroom after I finished brushing my teeth. "You were in the old house for a while."

"I told you. I lost track of time," he responded.

"How?" I asked.

Peter sat up in bed. The blank expression on his face didn't change, but somehow it felt even more removed than before.

"I was looking at stuff."

I let out a nervous laugh.

"Well, did you see any monsters in there?"

I'm not sure how long it took for him to answer me. It felt like the silence lasted forever and a day. When he finally spoke again his answer was short, succinct and to the point. He simply smiled at me, answered "yes," and then blinked his eyes.

I spent the evening in my parents' room after that, but I was too afraid to sleep.

In the morning Peter was gone. My mom and dad called the police. By the end of the day, they had filed an official missing person's report. His face was on the milk cartons and billboards. There was a massive statewide manhunt for him. Investigators believe that he was abducted so of course the press had a field day with it – the little boy who was taken from his bed in the dead of night.

The thing is, I don't believe Peter was abducted that evening by a prowler. I think whatever happened to him in the old house is what really led to his disappearance. It was my conversation with him before bed that cemented that idea in my mind – specifically when I asked him if he'd seen any monsters. His reply had terrified me more than words could ever describe.

It wasn't the grin he flashed before he answered. Though I found his smile disturbing, it's not what had captured my attention. Nor was it his response confirming that had indeed seen a "monster" while in the house. You see, the thing that truly frightened me, that sent me running to my mom and dad's room was what happened when he blinked his eyes. It scared me because when they closed, his eyelids shut the wrong way.

FREAK SHOW

The carnival rides' bright lights gleamed in the summer night like a sea of swirling, twirling, multicolored gemstones. Laughter filled the evening sky above the festive lot as adults and children alike took part in all of the fair's amusing attractions. The smell of buttery popcorn danced in the air, pirouetting with the sweet aromatic fragrances rising up from the carts of the cotton candy vendors. But amongst all the revelry and merriment, no one seemed to notice a young girl holding a pink balloon, and wandering through the crowd all by herself.

It was Elle's first time at the fair. The little girl was only seven-years-old and had tagged along with her older brother and his group of friends. From the moment she arrived, she had found herself mesmerized by a myriad of enchanting sights and sounds. The place was unlike anything she had ever seen before and she wanted to experience all of it. Elle's teenage chaperones, on the other hand, were only interested in flirting with every pretty girl they happened to come across so she snuck away when they weren't paying attention, hoping to take in as much of the carnival as possible.

Finally free from her boring brother, Elle explored the lot, her pink balloon trailing behind her while she bounced from one spectacle to another. She rode on the carousel, watched a clown preform magic tricks, she even fed a sugar cube to a pony at the petting zoo. To Elle, the fair was the most magical place on the planet.

After an hour or so the little girl parked herself on a bench to rest her legs. She watched with a smile on her face as a group of thrill-seekers staggered off a flashy spinning ride called *The Cyclone*. It wasn't until the last of them had stumbled away that a small tent caught her eye.

The nondescript little tent was easy to miss, sandwiched between two massive whirling rides decorated in dazzling lights. Curiosity beckoned Elle off the bench, taking her by the hand and leading her over to it. She stopped in front of the entrance and looked at the wooden sign hanging above her head. The words sent a shudder throughout the child's body.

FREAK SHOW

Elle had heard of carnival freaks before, but never thought she'd get the opportunity to actually see one in person. Intrigue and fear waged a war inside of the little girl's head as she contemplated whether or not to go inside. When the dust had settled, it was intrigue that had won out. Elle pushed the flap of the entrance to the side and ducked into the tent, followed closely behind by her pink balloon.

The inside of the tent was darker than she had expected. Off to the left, a tiny candle flickered on a table providing the only source of light. It took a moment for Elle's eyes to adjust, but once they did, she could feel the air escape her lungs as a sense of dread gushed through her veins. The little girl was staring at the most hideous boy she had ever seen before in her life.

He appeared to be suffering from some sort of terrible deformity that rendered his body a grotesque, tangled, bed-ridden mass of flesh and bones. His disfigured face, warped and misshapen, looked like a Picasso painting as the candle light flickered off of his malformed features. He opened his mouth to speak, but only a few raspy breaths escaped from his crooked lips.

"That means he likes you." Elle spun around to see an old woman covered head to toe in tattoos. The hundreds of piercings in her face jingled like a pocket full of change as she continued to talk. "Oh don't be alarmed. His name is The Human Pile and he's a member of our little family. I know we're not as pretty as you are, but we're just people and there's certainly nothing to be afraid of. I'm Tattoo Lady. It's nice to meet you."

"F-family?" asked Elle.

"Of course. There are more freaks here than just The Human Pile and myself.

Come on out everybody. The little girl wants to see you."

Elle swallowed the scream in her throat as more horribly disfigured people slinked out of the shadows and into the light. The old tattooed woman pointed to a man with grey scaly skin. When he smiled at Elle she noticed that his teeth were as sharp as a carnivorous predator's.

"That's The African Snake Man," whispered Tattoo Lady. "He joined our family two years ago. Travelled all the way from Liberia to be with us. Do you know where that is?"

Elle shook her head. The old tatted up woman let out a chuckle. The piercings in her face clanked loudly as it mixed with her laughter, making it sound almost mechanical.

"That's ok. Over there is The Tumor Woman."

The tattooed freak pulled a pocketknife from her waistband and pointed the blade towards a woman in a sundress. Monstrous cysts were growing from her unsightly face. She waved a swollen hand, covered in lumps and growths, at Elle, causing the little girl to wince.

"I think I wanna go home now," mumbled Elle.

"Nonsense!"

Tattoo Lady jabbed her pocketknife above the little girl's head. A loud *POP* boomed throughout the tent. The ribbon attached to Elle's balloon went limp in her hand. Her balloon was now nothing but a mangled piece of pink latex lying in the dirt at her feet.

"Come now," said Tattoo Lady. "There are more members of our family you must meet. Over there is The Lobster Boy."

A sneering teenage boy around the same age as her brother waved a pair of claw like hands in the air. The little girl could feel her heart beginning to race.

"And there," the old tattooed woman put her arm around Elle and pointed her knife at a man whose body was completely covered in fur. "They call him The Mongrel." A wicked smile crept its way across the old woman's pierced lips as she spoke again. "Now there's one more member of our family. Her name is The Little No Face Girl."

Elle shifted her eyes around the tent, but couldn't figure out whom Tattoo Lady was referring too.

"B-but there's nobody else here?" stuttered Elle. "Where is she?"

The old tattooed woman placed the edge of her blade at the top of Elle's hairline. A trickle of blood ran down her brow.

"Don't worry, child," she snickered. "The Little No Face Girl will be here really soon."

THE STRANGER'S DEBT

'Knock Knock'

The knock on the door startled Marie. It was too late to be expecting visitors. She had just put her son to bed. Her husband, Eric, was hunched over at the sitting area in the foyer with a glass of thirty-year-old scotch in one hand and his head in the other. He had seemed uncharacteristically distraught as of late. Marie loved her husband, but she realized she hadn't been very attentive lately. Between running her charity, attending social functions, and playing on the country club's tennis team she hadn't gotten the opportunity to ask Eric what had been troubling him. She knew his company's stock had recently dropped a couple of points so she just assumed it was a money issue. To her, a little bit of cash was nothing to fret over. After all, they had come from practically nothing and now they had plenty of it. They would be fine.

The knock came again.

'*Knock Knock*'

Marie tugged open the heavy oak door to reveal an ominous looking stranger standing behind it. He was so tall that he had to duck his massive head under the oversized door's 10 ft. tall frame as he entered the room. His skin was pale; almost snow white, a stark contrast to his intense shadowy eyes – two dark pieces of coal buried deep into the sunken sockets of his face. The stranger wore a long black trench coat buttoned down from his neck all the way to just below his knees. His hands and feet were massive – nearly twice the size of a normal man's. When he smiled at Marie she caught a glimpse of his teeth. Jagged and pointed, they looked like they belonged in the mouth of a mangy dog.

The stranger turned his colossal head towards Marie's husband and began to speak. His voice was low and gravelly, but so powerful she felt it rumble through the room's walls and her body alike.

"Eric Wallace. I have come to collect my debt."

It was at that moment Marie understood what was going on: The success of Eric's Internet startup, the big house in the hills, the fancy cars, the charity, and most importantly the horrible, giant, inhuman looking man who had just entered their home. Eric had made a deal with the devil. She flung herself to the demon's feet.

"Please! You can't take his soul!" she cried. "There has to be another way!"

The stranger reached out a long bony finger and caressed her wet, tear-soaked cheeks.

"Oh, my dear," he began. "I'm afraid you misunderstand. Your husband didn't sell me *his* soul. *He sold me yours*."

A NOVICE KILLER

I killed my wife last night.

I did it because she was cheating on me. Ok, so I didn't have any tangible proof, but every time she came home I could smell the cologne of other men on her. Try putting yourself in my shoes, slogging through the door after a hard day's work, and giving your wife a kiss only to inhale the scent of another man on her clothes. I mean, so what if she worked in the cologne department at Macy's? That's not an excuse! She was cheating on me, I tell you!

And I had enough of it! Nobody cheats on Phineas P. Woldsworth! That's not my name, but nobody cheats on me either! The point is, the bitch had to die.

I've never murdered a person before. I guess I always pictured it would go more smoothly. In the movies when someone gets their throat slashed they bleed a little then usually die a neat, instantaneous death. Quick and clean – that's how it was supposed to be. I snuck up behind her after she had fallen asleep on the couch watching Real Housewives of Timbuktu (or some other vapid reality show) then opened up her throat with a kitchen knife – she gushed like a geyser. You should have seen it! I didn't know a person's body could hold so much blood! I'm not ashamed to admit, I got a little light headed from the sight.

Well, it certainly wasn't a neat kill...and it wasn't a quick one either, for that matter. My wife fell to the floor after I sliced into her neck and began to wildly thrash her arms and legs. I'm sure she would have been screaming too if I hadn't done a number on her vocal chords. It took about a dozen more stabs to her windpipe before she finally stopped moving. I was kind of disappointed when I realized that the knife I used was a wedding present from my late

Aunt Carla. She was my favorite Auntie and that damn thing held a lot of sentimental value to me, but now I had to get rid of it. There was no way I was going to keep the murder weapon in my house! That would be crazy!

Once my wife stopped breakdancing on the floor, I looked around the house to survey the damage. Both our bodies and half the living room were completely coated in blood. I dragged her into my bathroom and dumped her corpse in the tub. The mess took hours to clean up, but I think I did a bang-up of a job. I got that living room looking like something you'd see Martha Stewart bedazzling throw pillows in. All I have to say is, *thank goodness for hardwood floors!* It would have been a *hell of a lot harder* if we had laid down carpeting like my wife insisted when we first moved in. I patted myself on the back for putting my foot down and nixing that idea.

After I was done cleaning, I went back inside the bathroom and tried to figure out what to do with her cadaver. I always do my best thinking on the can so I popped a squat next to her and began to make a number two. What? I didn't think she was going to mind?

I was just beginning to breech when I noticed something out of the corner of my eye. Her stomach had started moving – heaving up and down at an alarming rate. It startled me so much I nearly fell off the pot. *Was she breathing?* I felt a wave of guilt begin to wash over me. How selfish of me not to turn on the vent! A second wave smacked me in the face, but this time it was fear.

How could she be alive? I thought to myself. *She must have spilled enough blood to fill a dumpster!*

I tried to reassure myself that it wasn't what it looked like. I remembered once reading in a magazine that gas can escape a body, sometimes hours after death. This can give the appearance of breathing, but does not actually mean that the body is doing so.

Just as my heartbeat had returned to its regular cadence I could have sworn I saw her fingers twitch. The sight made me want to get up and sprint as far away from the house as possible – turtle head poking out of my crack and all! A scene from an old television show jogged my memory, allowing me to collect myself. In it, a crime scene investigator explained to a plucky young police officer that even though a person's brain may be dead, their body's muscles can still twitch for a little while after they pass.

See? I thought to myself as I pushed a little harder, trying to coax the chocolate bunny from its hole. *There is always a logical explanation for these types of things.* Sometimes things can't be explained though. I realized that when my wife turned her partially detached neck towards me and opened her eyes. The look of rage on her face made me want to scream, but I was too terrified to make a peep. She opened her mouth and I'll never forget the sound of her gurgling voice as it reverberated off the bathroom walls.

"LIGHT A MATCH!"

PLOP

WHAT WOULD YOU DO?

I suppose I always pictured myself curling up with my loved ones in a moment like this; tears trickling down our faces while we assured each other we would all be together again on the other side. For a second I wonder where my parents are and what my sister is up to.

As thoughts of my family fade away into the ether, my focus once again turns to the man, whose face I'm currently stomping into a bloody pulp. I can feel his cartilage and bones crunching under the heel of my boot. No one tries to stop me. Hell, there are about a half dozen other murders going on in the street at the same time. It's amazing how only six days ago people were shuffling through this intersection, briefcases and designer purses in hand, on their way to work. Now the street is alive with people fighting, screaming, looting – *even fucking*. I peer up towards the night sky and wipe some sweat from my brow.

It looks bigger than the moon now.

I marvel at its majesty as I drag my foot along the ground, wiping brain across asphalt as if I just stepped in dog shit. The eggheads at NASA are predicting that it should pierce our atmosphere and make impact within the next half hour. Experts are expecting it to wipe out 98% of life on Earth, but you don't need to be a rocket scientist to realize that when a rock the size of Australia collides with your planet, there's not much of a chance for survival. My eyes scan the scene, looking for someone else to kill or fuck. Who cares right? We'll all be dead soon anyways. Hey, don't judge me. Deep down you know you'd do the same.

NO MORE SINS

We met at a rally. Mamma always said that church was the best place to meet a man, but I was sure that he had strong religious convictions. *He was on the right side of the picket lines, after all.* I figured that anybody willing to stand-up to those goddamn harlots must be a man of the lord. Just the thought of those sluts choosing sin and debauchery over the life of an innocent baby is enough to make me want to upchuck. I can't stand the sense of entitlement some of the women who come in and out of that clinic, have. It's not your body; it's God's. He's just lending it to you, honey.

Sorry, I digress. We were talking about him, weren't we?

You should have seen him. He was so handsome – curly blond hair and the eyes of an angel. You could hear the passion in his voice every time one of those little whores walked by on their way into that slaughterhouse. I was far too shy to approach to him, but that wouldn't have been very ladylike of me anyways. When our eyes met I felt my stomach flutter. Even to this day, thinking about that moment still gives me goosebumps. He smiled at me and told me his name. I replied in kind and I knew he could tell that I was already smitten.

We began to court shortly after. He was always the perfect gentleman. So many men act like they care about you, but in reality they're only interested in getting into your pants. It felt different with him though. There was no heavy necking and he never pressured me to kiss him. Our dates mostly consisted of sitting under my favorite Juniper tree at the park while we discussed the book of the Lord. He was so knowledgeable. I fancied hearing all of his interesting thoughts and ideas when he talked about scripture. Once I even told him that he should write a book about the bible, but he laughed my suggestion off. He stated that people who buy that kind of literature weren't usually as open-minded as I was. It made me blush when he said that.

I think I fell head over heels for him before the summer was over. When you're in love, your heart makes you do funny things. Every time I saw him it became increasingly more difficult to control my urges. I wanted to hold him, to kiss him all over his body. I wanted to feel his hands caressing my breasts, but we weren't married and I knew that Jesus would frown on me if I acted on my desires. I was certainly no sinner, after all. Not like those sluts at the clinic.

I remember the last time I ever saw him just as clear as if it were yesterday.

He had walked me home from the park after one of our dates. We were discussing the book of Job, but I'm embarrassed to say that I wasn't paying too much attention. The demon, lust, had clouded my mind, making it almost impossible for me to focus. When we arrived at my front door, I asked him if he wanted to come inside for a while. I knew it was Bingo night at the church, which meant Mama wouldn't be home until late in the evening. He seemed surprised by my invitation, but politely obliged. I'm not sure if my intentions were innocent or not, but once I had him all to myself, I knew I couldn't subdue my yearnings anymore.

I kissed him.

At first, he was frozen with what I can only assume was shock. Plunging your tongue into a man's mouth is not the kind of behavior one would expect from a proper lady like myself, but despite his stunned reaction, he slowly began to warm to my advances. I wanted him – all of him, and he told me he wanted me too.

I held his hand and guided him to my bedroom. Together we undressed until our figures were just as bare and exposed as Adam and Eve's. He held me in his arms and I kissed him again. I knew that what we were doing was a sin. We weren't married, but at that point I just didn't care anymore. I loved him and I knew in my heart of hearts that we would be together forever.

He took my virginity that night. His touch was the most incredible thing I have ever felt in my entire life. I was lost in his embrace, my body sinking like an anchor into the deepest darkest depths of his passion. He filled my entire being with pleasure. The intense sensation built inside of me until I felt as though I was going to burst. And burst I did – our love erupted that night into a carnal, hedonistic explosion of sexual gratification.

When he finished he stood up from the bed and shot a handsome smile my way. I asked him if he wanted to lay with me a little while longer since we still had some time before Mama returned home, but he declined my offer to cuddle. It was then that my lover informed me that he had gotten what he came for. His answer left me confused and upset. I had never pegged him to be the type to use a woman for sex.

I begged him to clarify what he meant – to tell me that he wanted to be with me, but hearing my desperate pleads only caused him to throw his head back and laugh. His voice had transformed into something horrible and repulsive. The mocking chortles gushing from his mouth sounded like the howls of a dozen dying dogs all crying out together in unison. But that wasn't the only thing about him that changed before my eyes.

I could feel my heart rise in my throat as I watched his beautiful blonde hair fall from his head only to be replaced by a pair of twisted goat-like horns. His nose turned upwards like a boar's while his chin receded to the point where it was almost non-existent. He smiled at me again, but now he was wearing the grin of a serpent. A row of pointed teeth glistened in the twilight that had trickled into my room.

The revolting sound of bones cracking and flesh tearing filled the room as his body continued to contort itself into a horrible, disfigured form. By the time the noises had faded his feet had become hooved, his spine was bent and misshapen, and his body had almost doubled in size. He looked down at me – those angelic eyes were now as cold and white as porcelain – and I realized I had been deceived by the Morning Star.

The beast spoke to me. He told me that he wasn't interested in a wife; it was a child he wanted. Of course the son of the devil could only be born out of sin – a sin I had been tricked into committing. I could tell he took great pleasure in persuading me to stray from the righteous path. I begged him to take it out of me, but he showed me no mercy. In the blink of an eye he had vanished from my bedroom, leaving only the lingering smell of sulfur in the air to remind me of his presence.

That was two months ago. I've been worried about how I'm going to hide my bump from the rest of the church once I start to show. I admit that I've been tempted at times to head down to the clinic and get the demon's seed removed, but I made a promise to God that I would never sin again and I still believe that he will see me through this. I'm not one of those whores. I refuse to take the easy way out. God is testing me and I won't take the bait. As long as there is a child is inside of me then it's safe – even if I'm harboring the Anti-Christ.

TO MAKE AN OMELETTE

Daniel got into position and looked through the scope of his rifle. From his vantage point he had a clear shot of his target. This would be the second time he visited Nuremberg, Germany in the 20th century. The year was 1927, thirty-three decades before the time traveler had even been born. He had arrived to eliminate the menace that would bring about an unprecedented amount of death and destruction, the likes of which the world had never seen. The Nazi anthem began to play and a young Adolf Hitler would be stepping up to the podium soon. Daniel only had one shot.

He said a prayer and squeezed the trigger. His sophisticated sniper rifle fired a silent bullet through the air. The shot pierced the skull of the overzealous man aiming a gun out the window at Germany's future Fuhrer 100 yards away.

The threat had been eliminated. Hitler would go on to give his impassioned speech and rally the masses. In a few years Germany would go to war with the Allied Forces. The much more sinister, dangerous threat that would arise in place of the Nazi regime following Hitler's assassination would never come to power. Daniel let out a sigh of relief, looked down at his hands, and watched himself begin to fade from reality. Though he was terrified that his existence was coming to an end, he took solace in the thought that he had righted his past mistake and put the world back the way it was supposed to be.

THE PSYCHO AT RIDER'S LOOKOUT

Sheriff Riley slowed his police cruiser to a stop on the side of the empty road. The night was dark – stars twinkling in the black autumn sky above allowed for a little bit of visibility, but Riley couldn't see much beyond the reach of his vehicle's headlights. A wall of pine trees lined both sides of the street; behind those stretched miles of wild forest. He had received a call over his radio regarding a disturbance at Rider's Lookout, a scenic observation point located in the foothills mostly frequented by teenagers in need of a private place to fondle each other.

The sheriff leaned forward in his seat and peered over his steering wheel. Something moving in the shadows had caught his attention. It was the figure of a teenage girl. Her body hobbled towards the car like an undead creature wandering an apocalyptic landscape, on the hunt for human brains. Riley was able to see the girl more clearly once she stumbled all the way into the glow of his car's headlamps.

She was wearing a tattered purple dress. A matching clutch dangled haphazardly in her hand, swaying to and fro with each tired, haggard step she took. The girl had no shoes on – her feet were caked in a layer of mud. Her auburn colored hair hung in a disheveled, tousled mess. Riley unfastened his seatbelt and stepped gingerly out of the car.

"Hey there," he called out. "You ok?"

The girl wobbled over to the sheriff, collapsing in his arms when she got near. He propped her up against the hood of his car and shined his flashlight in her eyes to check if she was responsive.

"Girl? I asked if you were ok. You ain't been drinking, have you?"

"N-no sir."

Riley squinted. Dozens of deep cavernous lines bunched up around his eyes, as he studied the girl's face.

"Wait! I know you. You're the Wilson's girl, ain't ya? Bella, right? What happened?"

"Please, sheriff, you need to help me," cried the girl. Tears were welling up in her eyes, but Riley could see that she was starting to come out of whatever fog her mind had been drifting in. "He's still out there."

"Who's out there, girl? You ain't making much sense."

"The psycho! He got Buck."

The sheriff placed a hand on the rambling girl's shoulder in an attempt to calm her down. "Ok, hang on a minute. Who's Buck?"

“Buck! My boyfriend! He was my date to the homecoming dance tonight,” Bella started to sob, but continued speaking between sniffles. “After the dance we drove up to Rider’s Lookout. We were...we were...”

“You can spare me the details, darling.” Riley pulled a hanky out of his pocket and dabbed at the girl’s tear stained cheeks.

“Right. Well, we heard something outside the car so Buck went to see what it was. And there was a m-m-man out there! A maniac in a mask! Buck didn’t see him until it was too late! The psycho had a huge knife – like a machete or something!” The girl began to break down and started bawling again. “P-p-poor Buck!”

Sheriff Riley put his arm around the inconsolable girl. “There, there. It’s ok. So you’re the one that called the police, Bella?”

“Uh-huh. After he was finished with Buck the psychopath came after me. He chased me through the woods. Oh, sheriff, I was sure I was gonna die. He caught me and pinned me to the ground, but I managed to get ahold of his knife. That’s when I stabbed him in the foot. It startled him just long enough for me to get loose."

"You stabbed him in the foot?!"

"Yes, sir," the crying girl spluttered out. "Think it hurt him too 'cause he was limping pretty bad after that. He couldn't catch up to me."

Riley stepped back and scratched at the whiskers on his chin.

"You mean to tell me some kinda knife wielding psychopath chopped up your boyfriend at Rider's Lookout?"

"Yes, sir."

"And he was coming after you, but you were able to stab him in the foot and get away?"

"Yes, sir."

"And that he's been limping after you through the woods ever since?

"Please!" begged the girl. "Please take me home! We need to get out of here!"

"Of course, darling," responded the sheriff. "You're safe now. Why don't you hop in my car and I'll drive you back to town where I can call your parents?" Sheriff Riley helped Bella into the back seat of his police cruiser. "You done good, girl. Stabbed him the foot, eh? Who knew you were such a resourceful young lady?"

He flashed an approving smile to the girl as he closed the door of his patrol car, securing her inside of it. Bella watched out the window while the sheriff limped around the vehicle to the driver's side door.

SHE KNEW

Allison left the club without saying goodbye to her friends. She knew she shouldn't have had that last Cuba Librè. Her friends told her that they made the drinks much stiffer at the local spots than at the resort she was staying at and she was feeling a bit tipsy.

She knew she shouldn't have gotten into the cab all by herself, but the hotel was over 3 miles away and she could barely walk a straight line. It's not like she was going to try to stumble back along a bunch of streets in a foreign country this late at night.

She knew she didn't like the cab driver from the second she got in his car. She knew she should have taken Spanish in high school instead of French. Maybe then she could have understood what he said to her right before he started laughing. She knew she was being paranoid, but she couldn't help but feel in her gut that something was wrong. She knew as long as she made it back to her resort she would make an effort to drink more responsibly and not be so careless all the time, but she knew she was dead as soon as the cabbie locked the car doors and accelerated down the road past her hotel.

IT WAS ELLEN'S FACE

It was Ellen's face.

Ellen, the pretty girl who answered the ad and applied for the nanny position Barbara posted about on the Internet. From the moment she walked through the door, the single mother of two knew she would be a perfect fit for the job. Ellen was kind, courteous, and charismatic – everything Barbara had been looking for. She appeared to be faultless. Her smile beamed with the splendor of a sunset at sea and her voice was delicate like the music of a wind chime singing in a gentle breeze. Nevertheless, there was something else about the girl that had struck a chord with Barbara. It was only after Ellen had gone home for the evening that she was able to put her finger on it.

It was Ellen's face.

She reminded Barbara of her best friend from high school – a girl who had passed away at the tender age of eighteen. They had the same gorgeous grey eyes and Ellen even wore her hair in a similar manner. The girl was an absolute delight, but it was her face that had won Barbara's over most of all. Looking at it just made her happy.

The children seemed to love Ellen too. They usually didn't do well with babysitters, but when Barbara invited the young lady over to meet the kids, they took quite the shining to her. It warmed her heart to see her children connect with the girl. Her kids had been having a difficult time opening up to people after their father walked out on them, but they showed no difficulty in bonding with Ellen. When Barbara asked them what it was they liked about their new nanny, the little ones responded with glee.

It was Ellen's face.

It made them feel comfortable and safe.

The young lady came over to babysit for the first time a week later. Barbara was finally ready to start dating again and had lined up a dinner with a handsome doctor whom she had met online. She left Ellen her cell number in case she needed to reach her while Barbara and her new beau were at the restaurant. The kids seemed genuinely excited to be spending time with the pretty girl and for the first time in years, Barbara felt at ease leaving them in the hands of someone else as she headed out the door.

Her date went better than she anticipated. The doctor was a perfect gentleman and even more handsome in person than he was in his pictures. The two hit it off right away, laughing over appetizers and sharing funny stories while enjoying delicious entrees. After dinner the couple decided to stop off somewhere and grab a cocktail before going home.

They walked across the street to a trendy upscale lounge. Barbara had expected the bar to be buzzing with life, but when they arrived they found the place was dead silent. Everyone, from the patrons to the barkeeps, had their attention turned to the TV monitors on the wall. Barbara and her date focused their gaze on one of the televisions as well. It was a news segment that was playing on the screen. Barbara read the graphic prominently displayed in bold red font under the TV anchorman.

SUSPECT IDENTIFIED: CHILD HOMICIDE/ABDUCTION CASE

Barbara realized that the news story was regarding a child murder that had recently been getting a lot of attention in mainstream media. The single mother usually didn't have the time to pay attention to those kinds of sensationalist news stories, but everyone else was watching so she followed along with the crowd. On the screen, the TV anchorman looked solemnly into the camera as he began to recite the words scrolling on his teleprompter.

"...New evidence suggests that the babysitter, who up until this point was believed by authorities to be kidnapped, is now considered to be the prime suspect. Police investigators have concluded that she acted alone when murdering the child she was hired to look after then faked her own abduction. She is still currently at large. We are going to show you a picture of the suspect now. Please be advised, she is considered to be highly dangerous. If you see her, call the police immediately."

A picture of the suspect was brought up on the television screen.

Barbara felt her stomach drop.

It was Ellen's face.

THE LITTLE HOBO BOY

I followed the young boy down the street, under a freeway overpass, and through an alley. I knew he couldn't outrun me forever. After all, the baby bum didn't even have shoes on his feet! He was fast, but the little bastard had something that belonged to me, and I wanted it back. What a world we live in! I took my eyes off my bag of groceries for one minute, just long enough for me to pop the trunk of my car, and next thing I knew the little thief was running down the block with it!

I turned a corner just in time to see him duck into an abandoned building. I had him cornered now.

"You dirty little vagrant!" I shouted, "Give me back my groceries or I will report you to the authorities!"

I was mad, but as I entered the building, I felt my rage completely wash away only to be replaced by a sense of sympathy for the young one. The little hobo boy, still clutching tight to the bag of groceries he had stolen from my shopping cart, was huddled in a corner trying to comfort three younger children. They were all girls and their clothes were just as unwashed and filthy as the thief's. Upon closer inspection I could see that they were mostly skin and bones. The poor kiddies looked like they hadn't eaten in a week! My stomach began rumbling out of empathy for the children.

"Please Mister," begged the little hobo boy. "You have to understand, I did it for my sisters."

I waved my hands as a showing of peace.

"I get it. You're hungry. That's why you took my groceries. Look at how scrawny you all are! Why don't you just keep the food so you can have something to eat?"

"I didn't take your groceries for the food," said the little hobo boy. It was about this time I noticed that neither he nor his sickly siblings were looking at me. Instead their gaze was focused over my shoulder. "I did it because I promised the monster I could find it a heartier meal than my sisters and I."

It was then that I felt a warm breath on the back of my neck.

TO BE NORMAL

What would you do to be normal?

I would do anything. Sure, it's easy to look down your nose at me – to say that it's ok to be "special" or that we should strive to be one of a kind, but the difference between you and myself is that my uniqueness was unfairly thrust upon me. I DID NOT ASK FOR IT!!! So I did what I had to do.

Last night, I waited for my brother to fall asleep. When I knew that he was out, I covered his face with my pillow and pinned him to the bed. It wasn't long before he woke up of course, and once his groggy mind started to comprehend what was going on he began to thrash and kick like a wild man. I've always been the stronger of the two of us, but I'm not too proud to admit that it took almost every ounce of strength I had in my body to keep him subdued. Thankfully though, as his lungs became starved for oxygen, his hips started to buck with less force and his punches slowed to sluggish, tolerable blows. Eventually he stopped moving altogether. You should have seen the look of relief on my face when I checked his pulse to find that it was non-responsive. Murdering my brother was the hardest thing I've ever done; I loved him. Hearing his muffled cries seep out from underneath my pillow was scarring. I'm certain those last desperate pleas for mercy will stay with me for the rest of my life. But like I said before, I would do anything to be normal.

You see, my parents wouldn't have let us go through with the operation otherwise. The doctors said that separating conjoined twins like my brother and I could have been problematic. They told our folks that our organs were too intertwined and if they performed the procedure, one of us would have surely died. It was a sacrifice no one was willing to make – no one except me. Now they have no choice and as the anesthesiologist begins to put me under, I look at my brother's corpse, take hold of his cold lifeless hand, and smile because soon I will finally get the chance...to be normal.

Want More?

Make sure to check out Vincent V. Cava's:

Decomposing Head: Frighteningly Funny Tales That Will Rot Your Brain

Written by the authors of several Top 100 Kindle eBooks (in their darkly comedic and satirical genres):

Here you have found a book so foul, so repulsive, so horrifying... that you will undoubtedly find yourself running to the nearest bathroom in an effort to both relieve your bowels and scrub your hands clean of its putrid filth.

Though these attempts will be in vain -- just as the authors of this demented book of short stories have planned. I speak of none other than the intolerable Mr. Vincent V. Cava and his dimwitted pen pal, S.R. Tooms (the pair oftentimes billed simply as Hideous and Handsome). They have finally released this humorous collection of terrifying tales, despite the bitter public outcry which demanded these pages never see the light of day... and perhaps for good reason.

Inside this tome you will read such stories as the much talked about "Gas Station Bathroom," which has been known to cause many travelers to rethink their next rest stop pullover.

The psychological masterpiece in "The Horror of Knowing" will never allow you to gaze upon your friends in the same light again.

"A Favor for a Favor" depicts an unparalleled moralistic look at the true nature of mankind -- complete with an exquisitely satisfying finish that will have you shaking your head with sinister disbelief.

These are but a few of the many finely crafted tales lurking within this haunted collection. To those of you with a few screws loose in the noggin or those with a twisted smile (and crooked tooth or two), I bid you enter this haven of horror...

Dark Anonymous Confessions

They say that confession is necessary to purify the soul...

However, there are some deeds that are so **sinister, so wicked, that even the most remorseful admission of guilt is not enough to atone for them.**

From the mind of Vincent V. Cava comes his most twisted book to date! **Frightening stories told through the voices of those who witnessed them.**

These terrifying tales will **horrify and sicken you.** For lovers of grim, supernatural fiction, Dark Anonymous Confessions is a must read.

DARK TALES:

13 New Authors One Twisted Anthology

Thirteen of horror's newest and most talented authors have converged together to bring you one twisted anthology guaranteed to make your **skin crawl and your eyeballs melt.** From the jungles of South Africa to the busy streets of India, from the lights of Hollywood to the skyscrapers of New York, this book of frightening fiction was penned by **authors all around the globe.** Read if you dare, but don't say you weren't warned...

On A Scottish Night- A Nebraskan farm boy gets more than he bargained when he travels across the pond to Europe searching for adventure.

The Skinless Man- A child wonders if he's made a mistake after agreeing to a deal with devilish creature living under his home.

Little Black Bugs- The hilariously horrifying story of a home infestation gone terribly, terribly wrong.

The Rekindling- In a utopian future where death is no longer an issue, the Grim Reaper turns to his last hope for assistance.

and so much more...

Dead Connection

Reader beware!

The stories that lurk within the pages of this book will have you **cowering under the covers in fear**, praying that the shadows shifting underneath your closet door are nothing more than an optical illusion.

Delve into the depraved minds of horror's newest authors in this chilling collection of tales.

JOIN VINCENT V. CAVA'S MAILING LIST!!!

FOR NEWS, DEALS, AND EXCLUSIVE STORIES!!!

AND FOLLOW ON SOCIAL MEDIA!!!

FACEBOOK – TWITTER - INSTAGRAM

Made in the USA
Lexington, KY
19 November 2016